Jesus Shows God's Love

A voice from heaven said, "This is my Son, whom I love;
with him I am well pleased."
—Matthew 3:17

ZONDERKIDZ

The Beginner's Bible Jesus Shows God's Love

Copyright © 2013 by Zonderkidz
Illustrations © 2013 by Zonderkidz

Requests for information should be addressed to:

Zonderkidz, 3900 Sparks Dr. SE, Grand Rapids, Michigan 49546

Library of Congress Cataloging-in-Publication Data

Jesus shows God's love.
        pages cm. -- (The beginner's Bible)
    ISBN 978-0-310-74148-0
    1. Jesus Christ--Biography--Juvenile literature. 2. God (Christianity)--Love--Biblical
teacing--Juvenile literature. I. Zondervan Publishing House (Grand Rapids, Mich.)
BT302.J5765 2014

    232.9--dc23   2013027609

Editor: Mary Hassinger
Cover & Interior Design: Diane Mielke

Printed in China

21 22 /DSC/ 20 19 18 17 16 15 14 13 12 11 10 9 8 7 6 5

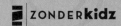

When Jesus was born, it was a special day.
God gave the world a great and wonderful gift.
Jesus was finally here and he was going to save us!

Even angels came to earth and sang praises, "Glory to God in the highest! Peace to everyone on earth."

Jesus grew up, just like everyone else. He lived with his mother Mary and his father Joseph. They taught him to be a good boy.

And Jesus grew up to be a good and caring man.

One day, Jesus went to see his cousin John.
John lived in the wilderness and preached about Jesus
to many people.

John also baptized people.
He said, "Get ready! The Lord is on his way!"

When he saw John, Jesus asked, "Will you please baptize me?"
John was surprised. He thought Jesus should baptize him.
But Jesus said, "John, my Father says you should do this."
And so John baptized Jesus.

Now Jesus was finally ready. God wanted Jesus to teach the world about love.

And so Jesus started work right away. "I will need some help," he thought.

Jesus found twelve good men to help him. Some of the men were fishermen. They left their boats and became teachers with Jesus.

Jesus said to his new friends, "Come with me. Help me teach about my Father's love."

And the men said, "We are happy to be your disciples."

Jesus told his friends about God.
He said, "Love your enemies, do good to those who hate you."

When they were all ready, Jesus and his friends walked and walked to many cities. They talked and talked to many people.

Jesus' message was always about love.
He said, "Love each other as you love yourself."

The disciples had the same message of love.
They said, "Listen to Jesus. He is here because God loves you."

People believed in Jesus' message of love. They came to him for help.

They listened to his words as he taught them to pray.
Jesus said, "Pray like this ... 'Our Father in heaven, hallowed
be your name ...'"

Even when Jesus and his disciples were tired, the people wanted to listen more to Jesus.

So Jesus and his disciples did not stop talking about God's love.

Their words and actions showed people over and over that God's love is for everyone.

And everyone, the young and the old that heard Jesus and the disciples speak, knew that God loved them very much.